Arrr, Mustache Baby!

BRIDGET HEOS

Illustrations by JOY ANG

CLARION BOOKS | Houghton Mifflin Harcourt | Boston New York

CLARION BOOKS
3 Park Avenue
New York, New York 10016

Clarion Books is an imprint of
Houghton Mifflin Harcourt Publishing Company.

hmhco.com

The text was set in Tweed SG.
The illustrations in this book were executed digitally.

Library of Congress Cataloging-in-Publication Data
Names: Heos, Bridget, author.
Title: Arrr, Mustache Baby! / Bridget Heos ; illustrations by Joy Ang.
Description: Boston ; New York : Clarion Books, Houghton Mifflin Harcourt, [2019]
Series: Mustache baby
Summary: Mustache Baby and his firstmate, Beard Baby, set out to be heroes on the high seas,
  but soon the lure of pirate treasure takes hold.
Identifiers: LCCN 2018035162 | ISBN 9781328506528 (hardback)
Subjects: | CYAC: Babies—Fiction. | Pirates—Fiction. | Mustaches—Fiction.| Humorous stories.
  BISAC: JUVENILE FICTION / Action & Adventure / Pirates. | JUVENILE FICTION / Humorous Stories.
  JUVENILE FICTION / Imagination & Play.
Classification: LCC PZ7.H4118 Ar 2019 | DDC [E]—dc23LC record available at
  https://lccn.loc.gov/2018035162

Manufactured in China
SCP 10 9 8 7 6 5 4 3 2 1
4500742099

To Johnny, Richie, J.J., and Sami Jeanne
—B.H.

To Rich, Dana, and Reginald Stauffer
—J.A.

Baby Billy was born with a mustache.
Baby Javier was born with a beard.
Usually, they were fine young gentlemen.

But occasionally,
Billy's mustache curled
up at the ends,

and Javier's beard
grew pointier.

Then . . . well,
ye shall have to
wait and see.

One day, Javier and Billy set sail across the seven seas.

As captain and first mate, they rescued shipwrecked passengers,

saved stranded whales,

and fought mightily against menacing sea monsters.

Day saved!

By and by, Javier and Billy floated off to become . . .

FISHERMEN,

EXPLORERS,

SUBMARINE SCIENTISTS,

ENTERTAINERS
on a cruise ship,

and finally,

NAVY SAILORS.

For trouble was brewing at sea.

Two pirates by the names of Captain Kid and
Short John Silver had stolen a treasure and buried it.

Javier and Billy vowed to give it back to its rightful owners.

Off they sailed for where
X marked the spot!

After digging and digging,

they at last held the treasure in their arms.

But just as they were returning it,

a strange ship appeared alongside them.

SHIVER ME TIMBERS!
It was Captain Kid and Short John Silver!

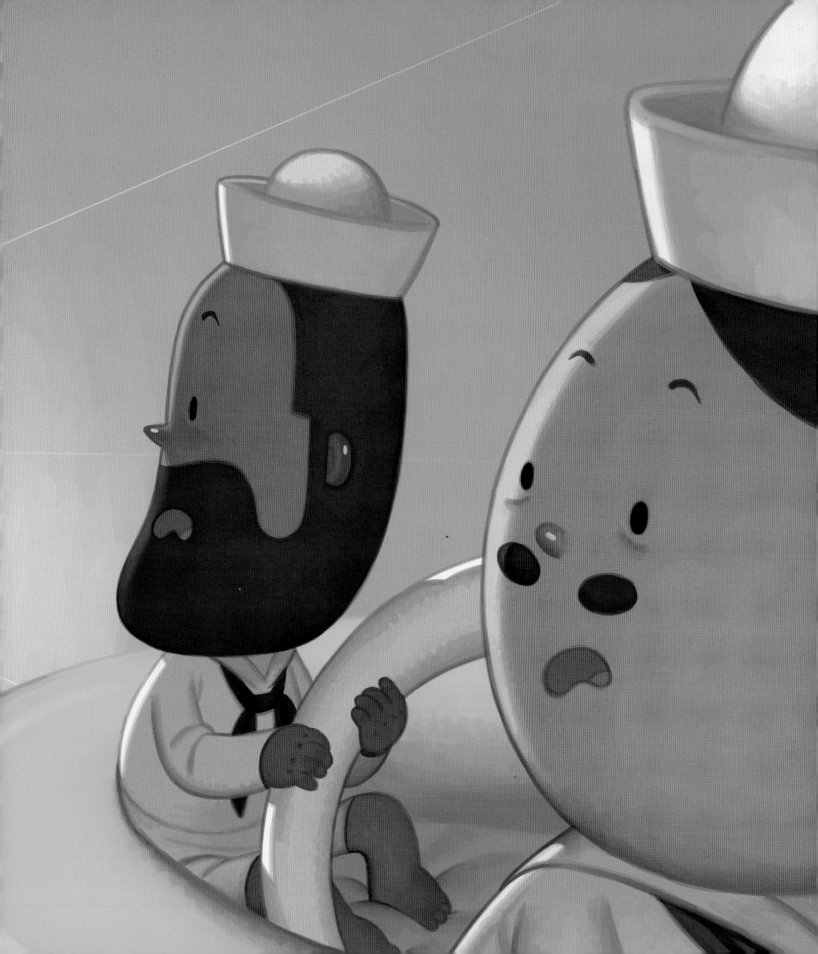

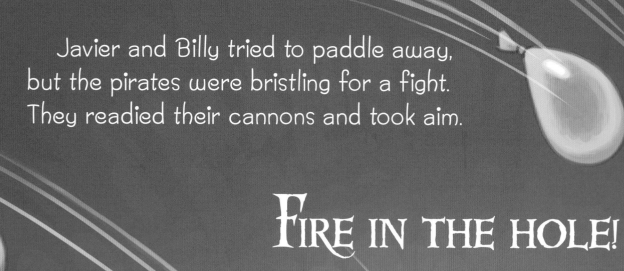

Javier and Billy tried to paddle away,
but the pirates were bristling for a fight.
They readied their cannons and took aim.

FIRE IN THE HOLE!

The pirates boarded the besieged ship
and demanded the treasure.

NEVER!

This was Javier's ship, Javier's rules.
No pirates allowed!
Javier challenged Captain Kid to a duel.

Make that a dual duel!
En garde!

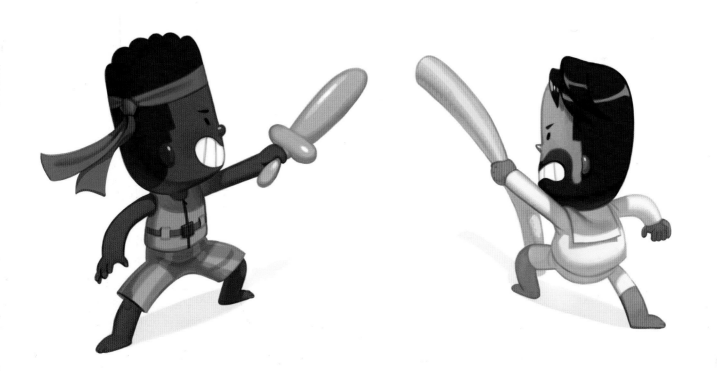

Billy and Javier were no longer playing nice.

With each swipe, Billy's mustache
grew and curled up at the ends.

With every swat, Javier's beard
grew longer and pointier.

Soon, Billy had a
BAD GUY MUSTACHE.

And Javier had a
BAD GUY BEARD.

ARRR, MATEYS.

They were pirates now!

Captain Kid and
Short John Silver
made a final lunge
for the treasure,

only to have it whisked away
by their whiskered rivals!

The pillaging pirates pinched the prize for themselves.
Now they wanted more, more, more!

The baby buccaneers sacked every sailor at sea.

Then the pint-size pirates dropped
anchor and looted the landlubbers!

What feasting! What fun!
Yo-ho . . .

...ho no!
So heavy was their ship
that it could no longer set sail.

AVAST!
The pirates were caught and forced to stand trial!

Guilty they were and sent to the dungeon!
Their cells were grim places, yet somehow
they managed to sleep, well, like babies.

When they awoke, Javier and Billy
regretted their raiding and ransacking.
They wished they could be heroes again.

With a little help, they made
a daring escape.

To show how s-arrr-y they were, they swabbed the decks,

returned the loot, and shook hands with Captain Kid and Short John Silver.

In time, the four became the merriest of mates, and sometimes . . .